NICKELODEON
DORA the EXPLORER ®

Dora's First Trip

adapted by Molly Reisner
based on the original teleplay by Eric Weiner
illustrated by Susan Hall

Ready-to-Read

Simon Spotlight/Nickelodeon
New York   London   Toronto   Sydney

Based on the TV series *Dora the Explorer*® as seen on Nick Jr.®

SIMON SPOTLIGHT
An imprint of Simon & Schuster Children's Publishing Division
1230 Avenue of the Americas, New York, New York 10020
© 2009 Viacom International Inc. All rights reserved.
NICK JR., *Dora the Explorer*, and all related titles, logos, and characters are
registered trademarks of Viacom International Inc. All rights reserved, including the right
of reproduction in whole or in part in any form. SIMON SPOTLIGHT, READY-TO-READ, and colophon are
registered trademarks of Simon & Schuster, Inc.
Manufactured in the United States of America
First Edition
2 4 6 8 10 9 7 5 3 1

Library of Congress Cataloging-in-Publication Data
Reisner, Molly.
Dora's first trip / adapted by Molly Reisner ; based on the original
teleplay by Eric Weiner ; illustrated by Susan Hall.
—1st ed. p. cm.
"Based on the TV series Dora the Explorer as seen on Nick Jr."
ISBN-13: 978-1-4169-6875-7
ISBN-10: 1-4169-6875-X
I. Hall, Susan T., 1940- II. Weiner, Eric. III. Dora the explorer
(Television program) IV. Title.
PZ7.R27747Do 2009
[E]—dc22
2008006160

Hi! I am .
DORA

This is my first time

exploring!

Will you come with me?

I see  !
FOOTPRINTS

I use my
MAGNIFYING GLASS

to follow the .
FOOTPRINTS

Who is here?

It is a monkey who

wears  !
RED BOOTS

His name is  .
BOOTS

Hi,  ! My name is  .
BOOTS   DORA

Oh, no! A sneaky fox wants

to swipe the from !

RED BOOTS   BOOTS

The fox is named .

SWIPER

 and I say,

BOOTS

" , no swiping!"

SWIPER

We stopped !

SWIPER

 and I meet the 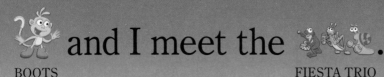.

BOOTS   FIESTA TRIO

The will play music

FIESTA TRIO

for the on the .

QUEEN BEE   MOUNTAIN

The  QUEEN BEE does not like to

wait!

Oh, no! The  dropped
FIESTA TRIO

their !
INSTRUMENTS

Will you help us bring the

 to the  ? Great!
INSTRUMENTS   FIESTA TRIO

The  is on the .

FIESTA TRIO   MOUNTAIN

We need to go through

the .

FOREST

and across the .

RIVER

 are falling in the .

NUTS   FOREST

We need to move fast!

 sees his friend  .

BOOTS   TICO

 will drive us through

TICO

the  in his  .

FOREST   CAR

Now we have to follow the

's trail.

FIESTA TRIO   BIKE

The trail goes

BIKE

through a .

TREE

Does the  trail go through
BIKE

the 🌳 or the 🌳?
CIRCLE TREE   TRIANGLE TREE

Yes! The 🌳.
CIRCLE TREE

We made it to the river.

This is  the iguana.
ISA

 wants to come
ISA

with us too.

We need a to cross
BOAT

the .
RIVER

 turns his into a !
TICO CAR BOAT

Which way do we go?

 knows!

We have to follow the

numbers 1, 2, and 3.

ONE   TWO   THREE

Do you see **1**, **2**, and **3**?
ONE TWO THREE

Smart looking!

Oh, no! fell into the !
BOOTS   RIVER

 the bull fishes
BENNY   BOOTS

out of the .
              RIVER

Thanks for helping, !
                                         BENNY

Now we have to get to the top of the .

MOUNTAIN

 turns his  into

TICO

CAR

an .

AIRPLANE

We fly up, up, up!

We reached the top of

the  .
MOUNTAIN

Here are your ,  !
INSTRUMENTS   FIESTA TRIO

The  can play

FIESTA TRIO

music now.

The  loves the music!

QUEEN BEE

Thanks for helping!

I love exploring and

meeting new friends!